SMYTHE GAMBRELL LIBRARY
WESTMINSTER ELEMENTARY SCHOOLS
1424 WEST PACES FERRY, RD., N. W.
ATLANTA, GA. 30327.

W9-AXY-277

WESTMINSTER SCHOOLS

Lindsy
Reed

PRESENTED BY

Jay Schroder
in honor of

Elaine Chestney
1990

SMYTHE
GAMBRELL
LIBRARY

DINOSAUR DREAM

Robin Michal Koontz

G.P. PUTNAM'S SONS · NEW YORK

for Shane

Copyright © 1988 by Robin Michal Koontz
All rights reserved
Published simultaneously in Canada
Printed in Italy by New Interlitho S.P.A.
Typography by Kathleen Westray

Library of Congress Cataloging-in-Publication Data
Koontz, Robin Michal. Dinosaur dream.
Summary: A boy who loves dinosaurs is taken
on a journey to their land one night.
[1. Dinosaurs—Fiction.   2. Stories without words]
I. Title. PZ7.K83574Di 1988b [E]   88-18171
ISBN 0-399-21669-3
First impression

3

17

Here are outline drawings of all the dinosaurs appearing in *Dinosaur Dream*. See if you can match the numbered drawing to the name of each dinosaur, then find it on the page listed.

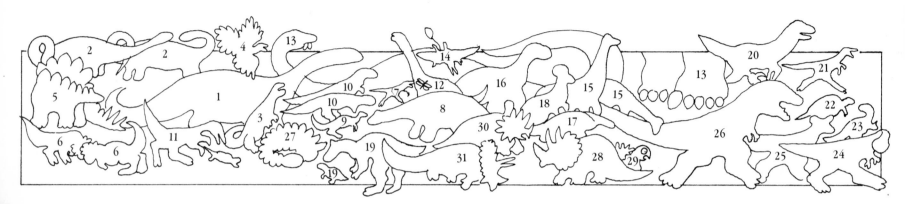

1. APATOSAURUS: "Deceptive Reptile"
   a-PAT-oh-SAW-rus (pages 10-11)
2. MAMENCHISAURUS: "Mamemchi Reptile"
   mah-MEN-chee-SAW-rus (page 10)
3. CATHETOSAURUS: "Vertical Reptile"
   ka-THEET-oh-SAW-rus (page 11)
4. ARCHAEOPTERYX: "Ancient Wing"
   ar-kay-OP-tur-iks (page 11)
5. STEGOSAURUS: "Plated Reptile"
   STEG-oh-SAW-rus (page 12)
6. PACHYCEPHALOSAURUS: "Thick-headed Reptile" pak-ee-SEF-oh-lo-SAW-rus (page 12)
7. COMPSOGNATHUS: "Elegant Jaw"
   komp-sow-NAY-thus (page 12)
8. AMMOSAURUS: "Sand Reptile"
   AM-oh-SAW-rus (page 13)
9. SALTOPUS: "Leaping Foot"
   salt-oh-pus (page 13)
10. CAMPTOSAURUS: "Bent Reptile"
    KAMP-toe-SAW-rus (page 14)

11. COELOPHYSIS: "Hollow Form"
    see-lo-FISE-iss (page 14)
12. BAROSAURUS: "Heavy Reptile"
    Bar-oh-SAW-rus (page 16)
13. DIPLODOCUS: "Double Beam"
    dip-LOD-oh-kus (pages 17, 18-19, 20)
14. RHAMPHORHYNCHUS: "Prow Beak"
    ram-fo-RINK-us (page 18)
15. BRACHIOSAURUS: "Arm Reptile"
    BRACK-ee-oh-SAW-rus (page 18)
16. CAMARASAURUS: "Chambered Reptile"
    kam-AR-a-SAW-rus (page 18)
17. PARASAUROLOPHUS: "Similar Crested Reptile"
    par-ah-saw-ROL-oh-fus (page 19)
18. CORYTHOSAURUS: "Helmet Reptile"
    ko-RITH-oh-SAW-rus (page 19)
19. MAIASAURA: "Good Mother Reptile"
    mah-ee-ah-SAW-ruh (page 19)
20. DEINONYCHUS: "Terrible Claw"
    DIE-no-NIKE-us (page 20)
21. STRUTHIOMIMUS: "Ostrich Mimic"
    STROOTH-ee-oh-MIME-us (page 21)

22. OURANOSAURUS: "Valiant Reptile"
    our-AHN-oh-SAW-rus (page 22)
23. IGUANODON: "Iguana Tooth"
    ig-WAN-oh-don (page 23)
24. EDMONTOSAURUS: "Edmonton Reptile"
    ed-MON-tuh-SAW-rus (page 23)
25. LAMBEOSAURUS: "Lambe's Reptile"
    LAM-be-oh-SAW-rus (page 23)
26. TYRANNOSAURUS: "Tyrant Reptile"
    tie-RAN-oh-SAW-rus (Pages 24-25)
27. ANKYLOSAURUS: "Stiffened Reptile"
    an-KILE-oh-SAW-rus (page 24)
28. TRICERATOPS: "Three-horned face"
    try-SER-a-tops (page 24)
29. PSITTACOSAURUS: "Parrot Reptile"
    SIT-uh-ko-SAW-rus (page 24)
30. STYRACOSAURUS: "Spiked Reptile"
    sty-RAK-oh-SAW-rus (page 26)
31. PENTACERATOPS: "Five-horned Face"
    pen-ta-SER-a-tops (page 26)